I0526972

Book Cover by Unfortunate Designs

Independently Published by Unfortunate Productions LLC

Print ISBN: 979-8-9913742-3-1

Clover Holloway

Slip Into Me

BLURB

Sara just landed the coveted last spot on a research expedition to the Caribbean, specifically the infamous Bermuda Triangle. But the position of a lifetime turns into a nightmare when their ship is unable to weather a storm of epic proportions.

Mitchell just turned thirty-five, which wouldn't mean much if he was human. Unfortunately for unmated eel shifters like him, the milestone means he has to return to the hidden eel city under the Sargasso Sea, giving up his shifted form as well as life on land.

When Sara is thrown overboard, Mitchell speeds to her rescue, only to discover she's his fated mate. Sara knows nothing about eels, shifters, or the secret underwater city, but it's a good thing she's a fast learner, because she just triggered his mating frenzy, and it's about to get really hot.

AUTHOR'S NOTE

I wrote this story back in December 2023, after I somehow won the Contest of Coital Chaos with a 500 word flash fiction story about a grandfather clock with three cocks. Several authors encouraged me to keep writing, and then my husband spouted a random fact about eels at me while we were in the car:

No one has seen freshwater eels reproduce in the wild. Once a year, all the adult eels swim into the Sargasso Sea (aka the Bermuda Triangle), and some time later, baby eels come out.

I took the idea and ran with it, intending to write a full length novel. But at about 10,000 words, I got stuck on the plot. I put it aside and moved on.

In February 2025, I discovered I was part of a charity anthology (it's a long story, but I didn't realize it until I was tagged in some instagram posts). With under a week to get something together, I dug this baby back out, threw on a mating frenzy, and hit submit.

As a Marylander, it felt right to base the beginning of

the story in my home state. I know it isn't a place known for electric eels, but this is also a story about a dude who can shift into an eel at will. Just roll with it.

All that to say, I really do enjoy this short story—despite its unusual journey—and I hope you do, too.

Stay lucky,

Clover

DEDICATION

*To Vera Valentine, who not only encouraged me to write more,
and who when I jokingly told her I should give this a clinch
cover, she said, "but what if you DID."*

Vera Valentine 1/27/25, 1:14 PM
Okay listen
But what if you DID

CONTENT CONSIDERATIONS

In case the clinch cover didn't give you a heads up, this story is an eel shifter romance with open door schmex scenes. It's pretty fluffy, without much angst, so if you're looking for a third act breakup, you won't find it here. Contents to consider include eels, eel shifters, a lot of swimming, incredibly smart women, masturbati0n, 0ral schmex, penetrative schmex, shipwrecks, near death experiences, drowning, fated mates, adult language, insta-lust, an over the top mating frenzy, a peen with unique anatomy, sexy scales and an epilogue with electroplay and foreplay in eel form.

CHAPTER ONE

T he first wet snowflake hits my head like a dollop of bird shit. Honestly, I would have preferred the poop. That snowflake means that it's finally nearing the end of winter, and the end of my time here in Cambridge, Maryland.

No more nine to five at the Blackwater Wildlife Refuge. No more Old Bay on everything or Snoballs in the summer. No more beach trips to Chincoteague with my friends to watch the ponies swim across. Not that my friends even really know me. They all think I got a dream job opportunity down in Jamaica. Well, I will be heading south for the foreseeable future, but it certainly isn't to jam out to Marley while sipping on some Red Stripe.

"Hey Mitch, can you help me dump these trash cans?" Roger's yelling quickly pulls me out of my thoughts. I don't usually work in the main building, but today was a "Lose the Litter" event—aka a day when it's all hands on deck so locals can come pick up trash to ease their guilt about single use plastics and shit. Yeah, yeah, *Save the Bay* and all that. My usual role here is patrolling the trails, marking where damage has been done, making sure there aren't any injured animals or illegal hunting and fishing. Generally, I don't run into many people on my route, and I prefer it that way. After dealing with 56 well-meaning volunteers for six hours today, I am all peopled out.

It's a mindless task, and I realize I've zoned out again when Roger stops abruptly.

"Hey, you ok, man?" he asks, "did you hear what I said?"

Looking at him, I wrack my brain, desperately willing it to tell me what Roger just said. Unfortunately for me, it's no use.

Awkwardly rubbing the back of my neck with one hand, I reply. "Ah no sorry, dude, I'm just so exhausted I must have spaced out."

Roger nods, some of the worry leaving his features. "Yeah, long day. I said that Marie was back again today and asking about you. I don't know why you won't give that girl the time of day. She is H O T hot. The jeans she had on earlier? Hoo boy, I popped a boner right there behind the desk."

"Roger, I really don't need to hear about your boner." The exasperation is clear in my voice.

"Look, I'm just saying, I haven't seen you go on a date...well, ever. You'd probably be less grouchy if you got—"

I cut him off. "Roger, I really don't need to hear about your boner and I really, *really* don't need any advice on my love life."

Roger holds his hands up in a placating gesture of surrender. "Ok, ok, jeez. Sore subject, I guess. Well, if you aren't gonna ask her out, maybe I will."

"Go for it."

Marie is a nice girl. She's a pretty, pert little blonde who knows what she wants, and what she wants is me. We went on one date five years ago when I first moved here, and she hasn't stopped turning up, hoping to give it another shot ever since. I guess it's slim pickings out here in bum fuck.

The problem is that Marie is *just* a nice girl. We had *an okay* conversation. I thought she was pretty, but nothing that stirred me below the belt.

The problem is that Marie isn't my mate.

I had honestly given up all pretense of dating, but when I ran into Marie at the market when I first moved here— and I mean literally ran into, with my cart—I thought it was some sign from above. Looking back now, I can see I was just desperate because I was quickly approaching 35.

Well, I turned 35 this year in August, which means I will be headed to the Sargasso Sea come December 1st.

Not ready to think about it, I push it out of my mind as I get into my truck to drive home. I need silence and a good soak.

The trip home is about forty minutes, but the drive is worth it. I love my little cabin. It's not much, but it's all I really need, and the biggest perk is that it sits on fourteen acres of marshland, so no one is going to just wander in. I need that guarantee of privacy, like I need to breathe.

Grabbing a beer from the fridge, I pop the cap and down half of it as I head down to the pier. The light smell of salt permeates my nose as I take a deep inhale, and I feel my shoulders immediately start to loosen. The sun is a vibrant ball of fire in front of me as the day slowly slips into night.

Placing my half-empty beer bottle on the pylon, I untuck my lime green polo that the refuge makes us wear before undoing my belt. Stripping down, I'm too tired to fold my clothes, so I drop them in a pile on the pier. Screw it. Who's here to judge me, anyway?

The water is chilly this time of year, but it barely phases me as I climb down the stairs and step in. Taking a fortifying breath, I do a shallow dive and as soon as my body is fully submerged, I start the change. It doesn't hurt like you think it would. That's magic for you, I guess. My body is now long and sleek, my two legs now a sinuous tail. I snap my powerful jaws and twist my body around and around, relishing the glide of the water against my skin.

Silence greets me, and I gratefully turn off my mind and just swim.

CHAPTER TWO

"**F**UCK!" Lauren's shrill voice echoes through the building and grabs the attention of all the researchers as she storms out of the station. Of course she's mad. I just clinched the last spot for the gig of a lifetime. Billionaire Edward Montenegro is taking only five crew members on his latest excursion, and by being the first to find the wreckage at the bottom of Lake Mjøsa, I just ensured I was one of them.

The ship at the bottom of the Norwegian lake has to be at least three hundred years old. Not quite viking, but the structures aren't modern either, indicating that the ship was built during that transitive period of modernization. It's a huge find because no one thought there was anything in this oversized ice fishing hole—Lauren included—and I just proved them wrong.

This find feels good, amazing even, but it is nothing compared to how I'll feel after uncovering the secrets of one of the world's most mysterious places: The Bermuda Triangle.

There are a lot of legends surrounding The Bermuda

Triangle. Stories of ships and planes going missing, compasses not working, and general bad juju. But I don't believe in magic, I believe in science, and science tells me there is a logical explanation for all the weirdness surrounding the Sargasso Sea.

Done with my day, I head into the locker rooms to take a much needed shower, cranking it as hot as I can get it. I left my wetsuit on the ship when we docked, and it's cold as balls here in Norway. It's like even my bones are frozen.

Why do people say that, anyway? "Cold as balls." I mean, balls are decidedly not cold, what with them being part of the human body and everything. Maybe they don't mean testicle-balls and actually mean snowballs? No, they definitely mean testicle-balls. God, I've gotta stop thinking about balls.

Stepping under the hot stream of water feels like I've died and gone to heaven. Okay, it isn't hot, per se, it isn't like this facility has a state-of-the-art water heater. At best, it's temperate, but after diving in the icy waters of Lake Mjøsa, it may as well be a hot tub.

Resting my head against the cool tile, I give myself a well-deserved minute of just sitting and letting the warm water sluice over my body before starting the process of shampooing and conditioning my hair. The hot water won't last more than ten minutes, and as much as I am enjoying this feeling, it isn't worth running out before I can rinse all the product from my hair.

After milking every one of those ten minutes of hot water, I meander to the dining hall for dinner. Everyone's eyes land on me as I walk in. Looking around, I see some faces who are looking at me with pride, and some with clear envy, before locking on green eyes filled with utter hate. Snapping my gaze from Lauren's, I look for Peter, who should be saving me a seat. I don't have the time or energy to deal with little miss priss right now.

Just as I spot him and begin weaving through the tables, a booming, slightly accented voice stops me in my tracks. "Ah, Sara! Just the woman I wanted to see. Come, come, sit with me and let us discuss your remarkable find."

Knowing damn well I am not going to refuse Edward Montenegro, I flash Peter an apologetic smile and switch directions to head toward the billionaire. Hobnobbing with rich strangers isn't on my list of fun activities, especially not as tired as I am, but to win, you've got to play the game. And I really want to win.

Edward pulls out a chair for me, gesturing for me to sit. "Please, Sara, sit, sit. I have been wanting to speak with you all day! Congratulations are in order!"

Sitting in the proffered chair, I smile up at him in thanks. "Thank you, sir. I'm honored to have been on the team that discovered the shipwreck."

"Please, call me Edward. No need for formalities here. Especially not since you will be joining the Lost Caribbean Expedition!"

His mention of the expedition perks me right up. That's the reason for all of this. All of my hard work, the lack of sleep, even the crumbling of my last relationship. Not that he was anything to write home about. The sex was subpar at best. This trip is the chance of a lifetime. The opportunity to unearth what no one has been able to. The opportunity to show my family, and the world, that the little girl who read pirate stories chased her dreams and isn't a failure.

CHAPTER THREE

Cranking the ratchet strap tighter one last time, I give it one of those manly 'that ain't goin' nowhere' flicks before stepping back to survey my jam-packed truck.

"That ain't goin' nowhere." Roger says, echoing my thoughts. Shit, men really are all the same, aren't we?

"Alright, thanks, man. I'm off. I gotta get on the road before traffic gets too bad." After a bro hug and a slap on the back, I climb into my truck and drive away from Cambridge forever. Everyone thinks I'm headed to the port to drop off my car and belongings on a cargo ship so I can have it all sent to Jamaica. The truth is, I'm driving to Miami. I'll stop at a couple of thrift shops along the way and donate my belongings, then pawn the truck off at some seedy dealership down in Florida. I can't just drive somewhere and donate the whole truck with all my belongings because let's face it that screams 'I need a welfare check,' and I really don't need to bring any attention to myself.

It's not like I can simply explain that I'm fine, but I'll be jumping into the ocean and swimming five hundred miles out to sea. That even sounds crazy to me when I say it that way, and I'm about to do it. No, it's better to just do it this way and kind of just...disappear.

A sense of dread settles like a lead weight in my stomach, and my chest gets tight. In less than forty-eight hours, I'll be on my way to a place I've only heard about in stories. A place I'll be stuck for the rest of my life.

HANDING the keys of my truck to the salesman feels so final. In a way, I guess it is. Nothing left to do but head over to Ocean Drive and bide my time until it gets dark and most everyone has left the beach for the evening. Maybe I'll just grab a bite to eat while I wait. It's going to be a long swim after all. Heading down the street, I see a little sandwich shop that promises the best Cubans in Miami. Well, when in Rome and all that. Maybe I can find a slice of key lime pie afterwards and really nail the cliche.

This restaurant embodies the definition of a hole-in-the-wall with a short service counter and several small tables squeezed tight together. It's loud, the aromas coming from the back are mouthwatering, and I know this is a great choice. It's places like these where you get the best food.

The line moves fast, and after a few minutes, a motherly-looking woman takes my order before I step aside to wait. It isn't like I'm in a hurry, anyway. Just as I settle with my back against the wall, the bell above the shop door rings out, causing me to look toward it. A group of five people step in, but it's the one in the front that grabs my attention.

She walks with confidence, all five foot two of her. She's wearing white shorts and a casually beautiful smile, like she doesn't even know how gorgeous she is. Her brunette locks are pulled up into a ponytail to keep it up off her tan neck. I'd like to wrap that pony tail around my fist while I—

Whoa, whoa, whoa. Where the hell did that thought come from? I'm not even into sex like that...I don't think. Maybe I am? Yanking my gaze away from the sweat droplets rolling down her nape that I'd like to trail with my tongue, I force myself to remember why I'm here.

I'm here because I am destined to become a mateless citizen of Ankaria. My kind are given until they are thirty-five years of age to try to find their mate, the other half that the Goddess supposedly made for them. If you are unmated by the time you turn thirty-five, like I am, then you must go to the hidden city and remain there for the rest of your life. That wouldn't be so bad, except you also lose your shifted form until you find your mate. You remain as some kind of horrifying human with scales, ensuring we can't leave without risk of being discovered.

Supposedly, it's nature's way of hoping that you'll find your mate there in Ankaria if you haven't been able to find them out in the world yet. It seems like a pretty stupid evolutionary trait to me.

Humans think eels all swim out to the Sargasso Sea to spawn and then die, and we just let them. Ankaria has been kept secret for centuries, hidden away by wards that deter any wayward explorers from entering. If they do somehow make it past the wards, either intentionally or by accident, they don't make it back out.

The stories about the shipwrecks are true. The lost planes are a stretch, but it isn't like we're going to correct them. Usually, the wards just kind of scramble your compass if you get too close, hopefully throwing you off course so you avoid the area entirely.

The only thing the humans get wrong is that people

don't just die when their ship is wrecked. We're a secretive race, but not unnecessarily cruel. They are brought down to the city where they live out the rest of their lives, sometimes even mating with shifters down here. They can never leave, of course, just like I won't ever be able to.

That's why humans never see anything but our offspring come out of the Sargasso Sea. Once an adult goes in, well, they are in for life. Like jail, except magical. And without the orange jumpsuits. And with a whole city to explore. Ok, fine it isn't really like jail at all.

"Number 56!" The loud voice calling my number pulls me back to reality, so I grab my sandwich and leave, giving one last glance to the gorgeous brunette before heading out.

CHAPTER FOUR

"Hell yeah! Now this is what I'm talking about!" Carla does a little happy food shoulder shimmy as she unwraps her Cuban sandwich. I have to admit, I'm pretty excited, too. Edward means well, but I can't handle any more fancy restaurants. Not only are the food portions the size of a snack, I literally do not have the clothes for them. I packed for an excursion, not dinner cruises and Michelin rated restaurants. Some good local food from a hole-in-the-wall restaurant is exactly what we all need right now.

Movement catches my eye and I catch sight of the man I spotted earlier, grabbing his sandwich and heading for the door. What a shame. I was hoping to secretly check him out some more. He was quiet, just standing off to the side patiently waiting for his order and seemingly lost in his thoughts. That worked out for me because it meant he didn't notice me staring at him.

The first thing I noticed were his bright green eyes. These weren't like any green eyes I had ever seen; certainly more striking than Lauren's, and those were her best asset.

Of course, after that I saw him rake his hand through his chocolate brown hair. Seriously, women pay hundreds of dollars at the salon to get that color.

I also didn't know I was into hands until then. I always read about women swooning over some dude's veiny hands in romance novels and never truly understood it until this random stranger. Hands shouldn't be that hot. They certainly shouldn't make me think about what they would feel like running all over my body. How it would feel to have them cup my breasts before inching lower.

Thank god our number was called before that thought went further. I shouldn't even be rehashing it now. Apparently, I'm just horny, but I have hands and my trusty vibrator for that. I've been giving myself my own orgasms for years and that isn't going to change anytime soon, especially not since we leave on our three-month expedition tonight.

Thinking about the expedition, I return to the conversation with Carla, Jake, Gustav, and Annie. Time to focus on this trip and getting to know the team I'll be spending the next ninety or so days with.

"I'm just sayin'. There is no way that man is straight. Have you seen the suits he wears?" Jake insists. Carla and Annie scoff.

"Just because Edward has fashion sense and enough money to get his clothing tailored—unlike you—it doesn't mean he's gay. What's it matter to you, anyway? You trying to lock down the billionaire?" Carla smirks at Jake, who blushes fiercely.

The rest of the meal continues much the same, friendly banter and lots of laughs. It bodes well that we get along already. Being locked on a ship for months with anyone can get frustrating, but if you don't get along with your roomies in the first place? Someone would get thrown overboard, and then we have to deal with all that paperwork...probably the news, too. Disastrous.

After we walk back to the hotel, we split up and head to our separate rooms. We have four hours before we have to be at the dock, so I'm going to take advantage of the fancy ass hotel Edward put us up in and take a luxuriously long, ridiculously hot shower. God knows I won't be getting one that nice on the ship.

The bathroom is high end, all white marble tile and gold fixtures. A tub stands in the right corner with a hole in the ceiling above it that water sort of just waterfalls from. I will never understand rich people.

The shower, though, is calling my name. Quickly stripping, my clothes are tossed unceremoniously on the floor before I eagerly turn on the holy grail of showers. The water is instantly hot. I moan in bliss as it runs over my shoulders and heats my entire body. In addition to the two shower heads and the massive bench, there are at least five jets spread across the wall to make sure you are never in danger of slipping out of the spray and getting cold. Fuck, this is heaven.

When I turn around, one of the jets directly hits my nipple, causing me to jolt in surprise. Once the shock has worn off, I realize I'm still horny. Is it wrong if I do a little self care? I'm not going to have a ton of private time on the ship. I may as well take advantage.

Turning slightly so that the jet hits my breasts straight on, I slowly slide my hands up my body to my breasts, cupping them hard while the water turns my nipples to sharp points. Closing my eyes to the sensation, my mind conjures up images of the man from the sandwich shop, the one with the sexy hands.

Is it wrong to fantasize about a man I don't know? Maybe. But what he won't know won't hurt him and I am too far gone to stop now. Sliding my hands back down my body, I imagine they are his strong hands drifting gently over my stomach, past my center, down my inner thighs, dragging his nails slowly back up along the sensitive skin. He drops to his knees and looks up at me with those bright green eyes, eyes that promise pleasure. As I imagine him leaning forward and pleasuring me with his mouth, I hold myself open with one hand and slide two fingers over my clit with the other. Fuck, I'm already wet. This isn't going to last long.

I just know that man would be talented with his mouth, and as I move my fingers lower and slide them inside of myself, it's his tongue spearing into my pussy instead. That image stays in my mind as a fingerfuck myself, trying to reach that spot that I know will make me explode and damning my short fingers for not being able to reach. I should have brought my fucking vibrator in here. This isn't my first rodeo, though, so I know how to make do.

Continuing to pump two fingers in and out of me, I make sure my palm grinds into my sensitive clit on each rough pass. Frustration sets in the longer I work my pussy. The trophy is so close, but I can't push myself over the finish line. Slipping my fingers out of my sex, it's time to move on to the big guns. You can't tell me whoever designed this shower didn't know *exactly* what would be going on in here because one of the jets is low on the wall. Spreading my pussy lips, I position myself in front of the spray and my pleasure instantly ratchets up to ten.

"Fuck, fuck fuck fuck fuckkkk!" Not even forty-five seconds later, I finally tip over the edge, leaning against the wall for support as I ride out the orgasm, thankful I'm not sharing this room with anyone. I wasn't exactly quiet. My legs are shaking. I haven't come that hard in a long time. Slowly, my breathing evens out and I turn off the shower, ready for a nap before we head out at midnight for the adventure of a lifetime.

CHAPTER FIVE

Mitchell

Midnight. I've put this off for as long as I can, but it's time. There's a pull I can't explain urging me to dive into the warm ocean and shift. Demanding I swim for hours until I reach our sacred city. It's the same pull that will guide me to the city's location. It isn't like I've been there before. Well, I was born there but my parents raised me on land so I have no memory of Ankaria. Unfortunately, this time the trip is a one-way type of thing.

I don't question the magic anymore. The outcome will be the same, regardless. Instead, I pull off my t-shirt and shorts, and hide them under some rocks in the cove. The warm water welcomes me as I walk forward, allowing it to creep up my calves, then my thighs, until I am deep enough to submerge fully and take my alternate form.

I'll never get over the rush that comes with shifting, and it makes me sad that this might be the last time I ever do. If I get to Ankaria and never find my mate, I will never regain my eel form.

As I start swimming, I see some lights above me,

heading out to sea. I have no idea why ships go out this late at night, but it doesn't matter. The only thing that matters now is the next five hundred lonely miles.

After about an hour of swimming, my thoughts keep getting more and more depressing. It's probably time for me to zone out and let my eel drive for a while. As this may be my last swim in my eel form, I'd rather just sit back and enjoy it, not worry myself into a panic attack. Not that eels can have panic attacks, I don't think.

The miles pass steadily until a humming assaults my body, yanking my consciousness to the front as I stop swimming. This is it. I don't know how I know, I just do. Again, I'm not going to question the magic. It looks like any old part of the ocean, but once I swim past those rock spires, I'll pass through the wards into what I've been told is a beautiful city.

Fortifying myself, I flick my tail to move forward before I can psyche myself out too much more. My body feels tight as I pass the wards, almost like a buzzing pressure along my skin. It doesn't hurt, but it doesn't feel great either. Once I'm through, however, the pressure immediately stops.

If I could open my eyes wide in this form, I would look like a child on Christmas morning when they see Santa brought them a new bike. Below me is what looks like a giant dome. Almost like a reverse snowglobe, with water on the outside instead.

I see others like me all swimming down toward some caves at the bottom of the dome, so I follow them. Swimming through the underwater tunnels is eerie. It's dark, but bioluminescent seaweed on the walls gives off an ethereal glow. It isn't long before I see light streaming down from the surface and the water gets warmer and shallower.

Instinctively, I shift and stand, peering at the incredible sight before me.

The shallow area gradually slopes up until it leads to a beach, where several men and women stand handing out towels and welcoming us to Ankaria. As shifters, we're generally comfortable with nudity, but it's nice to not be naked and vulnerable while trying to parse this new, magical place.

The streets are an ecru cobblestone, as are the stucco style buildings that line them. Brightly colored awnings and coral colored shutters give the entire place a vibrant vibe. Men and women bustle through what looks to be a market, browsing wares and running errands as if we were still up on land and not thousands of feet underwater in some kind of biodome.

Shaking my head, I grab a towel and mutter a quick thank you to the kind-looking woman who hands it to me, before heading toward the gathered crowd. I guess since they have to do this every year, they have processing newcomers down to a science.

"Good Morning everyone, and welcome to Ankaria!" A stocky man in a three-piece suit is on the stage in front of the crowd. "My name is Alton and I'm here to help you get acclimated. To your left, you will see several tents with purple coverings. After you're done here, you may head over there to pick up some clothing in your size. Once you've done that and are dressed, you may move on to the housing tents. Those are the tents to your right with yellow coverings. Each new citizen is assigned a living area in our apartment towers while you adjust to living and working in Ankaria. The apartment is furnished and stocked with everything you should need for the next month. I know it seems overwhelming, but I promise we are all here to help.

Now please, when you're ready, go ahead over to the purple-covered tents to get started."

Several pairs of wandering eyes look just as shocked as I am. It's reminiscent of the first day of college orientation. I'm just waiting on a bubbly TA to take us on a tour. Then again, what was I expecting? That I would just live on the street naked and hope things worked out? This is better, for sure.

As I make my way toward the purple tents, I see them. Mirrors. There is a mirror in front of each tent, and people are crowded around them. I hadn't really looked at anyone closely so far since we've all been trying to make it through this whirlwind of an experience, but now I surreptitiously glance around to try to see what our new forms look like. I glance down at my arms and chest, and see a faint glimmer in some areas. On the outside of my forearms, there is almost a strip of pale green scales. Another patch of scales starts at the tip of each shoulder, trailing down to my collarbone and forming a mottled V-shape above my pecs.

Unable to get a clear look at much else, I take a deep breath and walk up to a mirror to inspect my new form. More scales run up the sides of my neck, wrapping around the back. Slowly, I bring my fingers up to touch them, surprised when they aren't slimy the way my prior form was. Instead, these are almost like armor.

A breath I didn't realize I was holding whooshes out. When the stories were told to us, no one really knew what the hybrid form looked like. Of course, as young adults, we just imagined a horrible swamp monster looking thing that would terrify children. This form I can work with.

My gaze catches on some scales heading from my hip bones down, and I covertly pull the front of my towel away from my body to take a peek underneath. My eyes widen as

I catch a glimpse of my cock, which now has some bluish green frills under the head and along the bottom ridge. Well, that's fucking new.

"Next!"

Realizing I'm at the front of the line, I snap my towel back closed and step up to the cute redhead in front of me. She has on a name tag that says Mary, like she's just working the checkout line at Target. Normal day, no big deal. I'm sure she catches newbies checking out their junk all the time. Fuck.

Mary gives me a kind smile, then softly she speaks. "Hi, I'm Mary." She does a little point toward her name tag just in case I didn't see it the first time. "I know this can be overwhelming, but for now, just tell me your sizes and I'll grab a bag of clothes for you."

"Uh, Hi Mary. I'm, uh, a Large? Do you go by those sizes here? I don't...I don't really..." I trail off because what do I even say? *Hi, do you use normal American sizes or do you have some special Ankarian sizes I don't know about? Or do you use European standards? Do your clothes run small?* I'm not sure why this question is the one that nearly sends me over the edge into Panicville, but here we are.

Mary holds up her hands in a calming gesture, and I look back at her. "How about I grab what I think will fit and you can try it on, okay? I'm really good at this, trust me."

Unable to speak yet, I just nod and watch as she heads behind a curtain, presumably where they store the clothing.

She comes back a few moments later with a satchel. An honest to goddess canvas satchel like we are at the renaissance festival. I mean, I guess it's not like they can import Jansport backpacks, but still, it's a little surreal. Taking the bag from her, I thank her softly and she returns my gaze with a soft look. "It'll be ok, I promise. I know it's a lot. Just go on over there to the yellow tents and they will get you registered and settled in."

Nodding, I grip the strap of my new satchel until my knuckles turn white and head toward the other side of the square.

A man with green eyes like mine waves me over. "Hi friend! I'm Don, and I'll get you settled today!" He sounds like a cashier during Black Friday who is putting on their best happy voice so as not to scare off the customers. Except, I think he's genuine and I don't know which is more unsettling. Before I can say anything, Don continues. "I just have a few questions for you to get you registered, and then I'll give you all the information you need to find your new bachelor pad!"

Don gives me what I think is supposed to be a conspiratorial wink. Thanks for reminding me I am stuck here for the rest of my life because I'm still single, bud.

"Okay," Don draws out the word like it has 4 syllables. "Full Name please"

"Mitchell Abbott."

"Great, and your DOB?" Don continues to ask me question after question that I answer mindlessly. Height, weight, my former profession, what country did I come from; it all blurs together until finally Don sets down his pen and looks brightly up at me.

"Excellent, thanks Mitcharoonie! Here is a packet with all the information about your new apartment, and here are the keys. All the citizens of Ankaria are friendly, so just ask if you need help! Have a splendid day!"

As I go to thank Don—the happiest man alive—for his help, he's already looking over my shoulder for his next victim. Well, I guess there is nothing left to do but find my new home and try to settle into this insane reality.

CHAPTER SIX

Six weeks. It's been six weeks on this ship with no more company than the four other researchers and the middle-aged captain on this god-forsaken vessel. I've been on long expeditions before, but we always had a place on land to go back to at night. We've been at sea for six long weeks with no sign of anything unusual.

The only thing that's stood out is the fact the nautical compass on the helm of the ship goes haywire occasionally, and the team and I have decided that means we're close. But every time we think we are making headway, it seems like we get turned around.

Suddenly, sounds of yelling reach my ears, but before I can leave my cabin to investigate, the ship pitches violently and I'm slammed against the wall. Righting myself, I make my way to the door and fling it open, heart stopping when I realize a freak storm has come out of nowhere, and the swells around the ship are at least thirty feet high.

That shouldn't even be possible. What the fuck is happening?

Forcing my legs to move, I wobble unsteadily toward

the bow of the ship where the panicked voices are coming from. Annie sees me and comes darting over, the fear obvious in her eyes. "Sara! Oh, my god. This storm...it came out of nowhere. The captain says the ship isn't built for these types of waves!"

Saying nothing, I turn toward the helm and see that the captain is calm as he sits behind the wheel without attempting to right the boat. That's when I know we're about to die. A captain always goes down with his ship, right? And this one has decided there is nothing he can do.

The boat pitches again, and I grab the railing before I hit the deck. We are cresting a swell, and as we go over, the bow of the ship pitches sharply downward. Just as the ship rights itself, we all look up to see the next swell is too close and far too large. The ship is at an angle that will hit it dead on.

Closing my eyes, I take a deep breath as the water hits me and everything goes black.

CHAPTER SEVEN

T he screech of the siren jolts me awake and I shoot up off my cot, only to slam my head into the bunk above me. Each of the citizens of Ankaria is required to serve one shift per week at the emergency station. Since the magic protecting our city occasionally causes shipwrecks, we are on call to help rescue anyone who was on board and bring them back to the city. In the six weeks I've been here, I've never heard the siren go off. Of course, it had to go off today during my mandatory shift.

No need to panic, just get up and grab an oxygen mask in case you end up finding a poor human out there in the water. Breathe in, now out. I try to calm my racing brain, but it's no use. This is terrifying.

Dashing out into the common area, Gabe's already heading toward the underwater cave entrance that connects to the station. Following him, I dive in and swim as fast as I can out of the cave system and into the great open sea.

There are ten of us on call today, but only eight who go

out and attempt to find any lost humans. The two others stay behind and prep the medical bay.

Still following Gabe, I kick my legs harder and aim for the surface. Even though I lost my shifted form, the water gliding across my skin is still comforting. It's a miracle that this weird hybrid form still allows us to swim and breathe underwater, but I guess Mother Nature knew taking away the sea entirely would drive us to extinction.

Up ahead, a glimmer catches my eye. Swimming closer reveals it's part of the ship that must have crossed the wards and met its doom. Avoiding the wreckage, I sweep my gaze around, looking for anyone to help.

That's when I see it. A mess of dark brown hair floating just past the wreckage I just swam around. My heart jumps to my throat because I just know it's her, the woman from the sandwich shop. I don't know why I'm so certain, I just am. I haven't been able to get her out of my head the whole time I've been here. Maybe the instincts that guided me to Ankaria are now telling me she's important.

Pushing myself faster to reach her, I swim faster than I ever have before and grip her around her delicate waist. Pushing her hair back confirms what my gut already knew. I don't have time to question the fates right now, I simply cradle her to my chest and start to swim back to the tunnel, feeling a zing of awareness shoot up my spine when I have her in my arms.

No. No no no no no. This can't be happening.

The feeling of rightness alongside the heat of connection flares to life inside me, and I know this is my mate. My mate, who is currently floating lifelessly in my arms, jaw slackened, and eyes closed.

It's too late to use the portable oxygen tank. I have to get her back to the emergency station. Now. If I thought I swam fast before, it's nothing compared to the speed I'm employing now, even while dragging my mate's extra weight with me.

I refuse to have found my mate only to have her die in my arms two minutes later. The Goddess can't be that cruel.

Finally entering the tunnels, I curse the twists and turns that slow me down. Busting through the water's surface, other Eelkin gawk at me running full bore with a limp human in my grasp. Water trails behind me as I enter the med bay, a disapproving look on Dr. Pekrah's face glaring at it until I open my mouth and beg.

"Please! My mate. There was a shipwreck, and she...I—" Breaking off with a choked sob, the doc rushes to me, directing me to lay her on the table. He points to a set of chairs away from the exam area, silently urging me to sit there. He knows I won't leave if she's really my mate, but I do understand he needs room to work. Wandering over to the chairs, I find myself pacing, biting my thumb nervously as I wait.

THE FEELING of helplessness hasn't left me since I brought the gorgeous dark-haired woman to the emergency station and demanded someone help her. I don't even know her name, but I can't leave her side.

It's only been forty eight hours since I found her, but it feels like it's been weeks. The waiting has been tortuous and I need her to wake up. I need to look into those chocolate eyes and see life in them. I need to hear her voice more than I need air to breathe.

The nurses know what's happening. It's not like I've

tried to hide it. It's unusual for one of my kind to find their mate so soon after arriving in Ankaria, but it has happened. The only thing keeping me sane is the soft rise and fall of her chest, letting me know she's still breathing. Suddenly her eyes begin to twitch and I sit up straighter in my chair, my own eyes unblinking. Is she waking up?

Scooting closer to the bed, I lean over and reach out to grab her hand. As soon as I touch her, the strange yet familiar heat shoots up my arm. It's a feeling I've become accustomed to, even though it's strange.

This time though, something decidedly less comforting happens when I touch her. Her eyes pop open, and she screams.

CHAPTER EIGHT

There is a fish-man standing over me. What the actual fuck.

I thought I died, but clearly I haven't if I'm sitting here screaming my throat raw while a fish-man tries to calm me down. Or maybe I have and this is hell and I'm here because I didn't believe in heaven and all that shit. It would serve me right that my hell would have fish-men in it after spending so much time diving for lost treasure.

Two fish-women come running in, and the fish-man jumps back, his hands going up in a gesture that belies innocence. The shorter of the women glares at him, while the taller one slowly approaches me.

"Hey, hey, it's okay. No one here is going to hurt you. You're okay." Her voice is the same one you'd speak to a scared, injured animal in, but it works. I stop screaming, though my breathing hasn't slowed down one bit. The woman's smooth voice pulls my gaze back to her, and she continues. "My name is Martha, and that's Layla," she says, pointing at the other woman. "The ship you were on sank in a horrible storm. Our rescue team brought you in just in time."

The only thing I can do is stare blankly at her as I attempt to process this information. Finally, I gather enough words to ask where I am. I'm sure there is more I need and want to ask, but at the moment my brain is only firing on half a cylinder and this information seems the most pressing.

It's Layla that replies this time, "You're in Ankaria, the city under the Sargasso Sea."

Whipping my head around toward the shorter woman, I widen my eyes at her. "UNDER the sea? What is this, the fucking Little Mermaid? Where's Sebastian? The band of musical fish? Do I get assigned a talking fish sidekick? I have to be hallucinating." I mumble that last part under my breath, but I'm sure they heard me, anyway.

Huffing a deep sigh, Martha pats my hand in a motherly gesture. "I know this is a lot to process, but I promise it will make more sense in time. For now, just try to rest."

With that, she turns and leaves with Layla following close behind. As soon as the door shuts behind them, I turn back to the fish-man that was holding my hand when I awoke. Except now that I am looking at him closer, he looks oddly familiar.

I also see that he isn't really a fish-man at all. He has patches of scales, yes, but he's giving off more merman vibes than fish vibes. He stands shyly in the corner and lets me peruse him. Starting with his chocolate brown hair, thick and lush, it shines like he belongs in a shampoo commercial. He has small patches of greenish/blue scales on each temple and along the sides of his neck. More are peeking out from the collar of his shirt as well. I have to admit, he's kind of hot. You can tell he's lean but muscular even through his loose t-shirt. The scales run in a line down the outside of his forearms to the tops of his hands, stopping after forming a loose v-shape.

He self consciously flexes those hands and a bolt of heat shoots to my core. Damn, his hands are sexy. Wait.

My eyes fly back up to his, and sure enough, I'm met with the brightest green eyes I have ever seen.

"It's you."

His face turns red, and he shifts awkwardly on his feet. Before he can say anything, I continue, "I saw you in that sandwich shop in Miami. I know I did. How are you here? Who are you? *What* are you?"

Cautiously, he moves two steps closer to my bed, clearly not wanting to startle me after the screamfest that ensued when I awoke.

His voice is soft when he speaks. "My name is Mitch.Uh Mitchell, but you can call me Mitch. Everyone else does. Except for Don, he called me Mitcharoonie, which was just weird, but..."

His nervous rambling trails off and not only is it cute, but it puts me more at ease. No one who was planning to murder and eat me would be shy and nervous, right?

I mean, I assume if these people wanted to eat me, they wouldn't have saved me and healed me. The logic of that calms me further and I beckon for Mitch to come closer. "It's ok, I won't freak out, you can come closer. I have so many questions. I'm Sara."

He approaches cautiously, "Hi Sara. Um, is it ok if I sit?"

"Yes, Mitch, please sit. I'm sorry for screaming in your face. It was a bit of a shock."

"Oh no, I'm sorry I scared you. I really didn't mean to. I just needed to be near you."

He must realize how creepy that sounds because he

forges on before I can respond. "You said you have a lot of questions. How about I give you a little rundown of where you are, and what we are, and we go from there?" I nod and he continues. "Well, like Martha said, you were in a ship-wreck. You and the rest of the crew were thrown into the sea and we rescued you and brought you here to Ankaria. As for what Ankaria is…well, it's basically the secret eel city. I'm not sure what your ship was doing near the Bermuda Triangle, but our wards protect us by throwing intruders off course. Should a vessel get through, however, like yours did, well…."

He shrugs his shoulders and gestures around the room sheepishly, indicating that these wards or whatever caused my ship to sink. "Wait, you said the rest of my crew is alive?"

"Yeah, they're each in their own room here in the emergency station. All five others."

That's a relief, but then something else clicks. He said "eel city." Martha said we were under the Sargasso Sea. Back in college, I remember learning that we have no idea how eels reproduce in the wild.

Once a year, eels migrate from literally all over the world to the Sargasso Sea, which is inside the infamous Bermuda Triangle. Adult eels go in, and baby eels come out. Scientists have gotten eels to reproduce in captivity, but no one has seen the act in nature. It's generally assumed they go there to spawn, then die. Is he saying what I think he's saying?

"Are you saying…that you're an eel? That's why you have scales? But…you're human, uh, ish?"

"Well, kind of, yeah. I'm—we're—eel shifters."

Horrified, I ask, "are all eels actually people?" I can't

help but think back to all the sushi I've eaten and start to feel a little sick.

His eyes widen when he realizes what's going through my mind and he rushes to reassure me. "No! No, not ALL eels are eel shifters. A lot, yes, but there are some eels that are just fish. You likely haven't, um, eaten anyone by accident. We generally stay in our human forms unless we know it's totally safe to shift."

That makes me feel marginally better. "Can I see you shift?" I'm not sure what the hell made me ask that instead of one of the million other questions bouncing around in my head, but I have the strongest urge to see Mitch in his eel form. I want to experience this fantastical phenomenon.

Looking down at his feet, he shakes his head sadly. "I...I can't shift anymore."

"Why?"

"Well, for eel shifters, if you haven't found and bonded with your mate by the time you turn thirty-five, you must come back here to Ankaria and you lose your full eel form. You become an Eelkin which is...well...this." He motions to the general area of himself. "I turned thirty-five five months ago."

So that means he's single? *Whoa, down girl.* I mentally bitchslap my pussy for getting excited about that. This is not the time.

"I'm really sorry Mitch. Is there still a chance you could find your mate?" I didn't think he could look any more awkward, but he does, rubbing the back of his neck with one hand.

"Um, yeah. I kind of already did."

A crushing feeling hits my chest. Part of me is glad for Mitch because he looked so sad before, but the other part of me is jealous of whoever this mate of his is. What the hell? I saw this dude for forty-five seconds in a random sandwich shop. It isn't like I know him. Pushing that aside, I squeak out, "Oh, that's super great, Mitch!"

Mitch gives me a wry smile that turns into a grimace when he speaks again. "Um, Sara? I should probably just go ahead and rip the bandaid off here. It's you."

Halt. Back up. Do not pass go, do not collect $200. What the fuck did he just say? Looking into his clear green eyes, all I see is earnest hope. The only thing I hear after that is my own hysterical laughter before I black out again.

CHAPTER NINE

Mitchell

Sara. The sound of my mate's voice curls around my soul. I never really realized how sappy I could be before now. Who even am I? Roger was right. I *was* grumpy.

I didn't mean to freak her out so badly that she passed out again, but I thought it would be better to get it all out at once. I'm already drawn to her, and the longer I go without claiming her, the more intense my need will be for her. My cock is already at half mast and has been the entire time I've been in her proximity.

Seeing as I've already scared my mate so much she woke up screaming—and then passed out after I told her she's mine—it's probably best if I give her some space even if I don't want to. Seems like a good time to take a shower and change anyway, now that I know she isn't gonna die. No need to horrify her with my B.O. as well.

Taking one last look at Sara, I leave her room and wave at Martha and Layla as I head out of the emergency station.

I haven't been home since my shift started and I rescued Sara, but my apartment is exactly how I left it. A dirty cereal bowl in the sink, an unfolded blanket on the small couch; it's not messy per se, but it isn't exactly tidy. I'm definitely going to have to clean up before I bring Sara here.

If she even wants to come here. Shower first, plan of attack to woo Sara after.

Turning on the shower, I leave it slightly cold in the hopes it will kill this half boner I still have. It makes my whole body tense when I step under the spray of the water. "Sonofabitch!"

Going about my routine, I'm just rinsing off my body when I realize my erection isn't going to go down without some assistance. Dropping my hand to my cock, I give it one swift tug and then give in. One thing I've realized about these new additions to my member is that they feel phenomenal. Stroking up and down my length, I let my fingertips drag over the long frill that runs up the thick vein on the underside of my cock.

"Fuck." My hand moves faster and I close my eyes as the pleasure starts to take over. Not surprisingly, my mind conjures up images of my mate. Her scent, those big brown eyes, those plush pink lips I'd like wrapped around my cock. I imagine her in the shower with me, on her knees, licking up my bottom frill before circling the head of my cock with her tongue, flicking the frills on the underside of the head on each pass. Finally, she takes me inch by inch into her warm, wet mouth, pushing until her nose hits my pubic bone. When she starts to gag, I wrap that thick hair around my fist and pull her off my dick until she's just got the tip in her mouth, then I guide her in the rhythm I want. She moans around my cock and—"Fuck!" Bracing my hand against the wall, I come all over the tile with a shout, but my dick's still hard. Goddess, please let my mate accept me soon. This insatiable need is gonna kill me.

After a shower, another orgasm, and some cereal for dinner, I head back to Sara. When I get to her room, she's sitting on the bed, dressed in new clothing and seemingly waiting for something. She sees me enter and stands.

"So, while you were gone, the girls explained the situation more, and that I am never allowed to leave Ankaria. I can't say I'm happy about that, or accept it, but I need to get out of this room. They said I can stay in the refugee lodge, or they suggested I stay with you. I really could use a friend right now, and for some reason, you make me feel safe. Are you cool with a temporary roommate?"

I don't think I've felt a range of emotions so quickly in my life. Relief that she was awake, fear that should would try to leave, elation at the fact I make her feel safe, lust at the thought of having her in my home, and finally fear that I'll fuck it up. The emphasis on roommate instead of simply mate didn't escape me either. She's waiting for a response, so I quickly follow up. "Yes! Yes, of course you can stay with me. I'd lo—really like that."

Smiling, she comes to where I'm standing and reaches out to grab my hand. As soon as we touch, that bolt of pleasure zings through me and it's like I didn't just rub one out twenty minutes ago. She inhales sharply, her pupils widening. Does she feel it, too? She isn't Eelkin, but she must feel some part of the mate bond for her to accept the situation so easily.

As we walk up the street, I point out the market and other various landmarks. I've only been here six weeks, but the underwater city isn't exactly huge. She doesn't say much, just takes it all in and occasionally asks questions about the city or the people who live here. By the time we get to my building, we are walking in silence, but the tension is so thick you could cut it with a knife.

Climbing up the two flights of stairs isn't made any easier by my yet again hard cock. This should have been in the orientation packet: "What to do if you find your mate and they are human. How to stop your raging hard-ons and avoid fucking your mate in public." I'll have to take this up with Don.

Entering my apartment, she looks around, making me thankful I tidied up before I left. "Cute." She says, as she explores further. Well, she didn't say it was gross, so that's a good start.

Following her down the hall, I hurry to reassure her. "There is only one bedroom, so you can sleep there and I'll take the couch." Part of me wants her to tell me we can share the bed, but she nods and says, "Thanks. Um, could I take a shower? I was on that ship for six weeks and I haven't had a real shower the whole time."

"Oh yes, of course, here." I grab her a fresh towel and point toward the bathroom. "Feel free to use anything you want. I'll go set up the couch and find us something to eat."

"Thanks, Mitch." As she closes the bathroom door behind her, all I can think about is how it felt to hear my name on her tongue. And how badly I want to make her moan it instead. Fuck, this is going to be torture.

When I hear the shower turn on and the curtain pull shut, I set a spare blanket and pillow on the couch that will serve as my bed for the foreseeable future. There isn't much to eat in this place since I live alone and eat cereal as a meal more often than I'd like to admit. Right now, the simmering threat of the mating frenzy makes me not want to eat anything but Sara's pussy.

Too soon, Sara exits the bathroom, a cloud of steam rolling out behind her. She's wrapped in nothing but the towel, her wet brown locks even darker and pulled over her shoulder. The water drips from the ends of her hair down her chest, and I bite my lip to keep a moan from escaping. I want to trace that water droplet with my tongue. She steps closer and I realize she used my body wash so she smells like me, too. A small groan does escape me then, but she either doesn't hear it or chooses to ignore it.

Stopping about three feet from me, she admits, "I'm actually too tired to eat. Would it be okay if I just crashed early? And borrowed a shirt to sleep in?"

Imagining her in my shirt, in my bed, wet like she is now, is testing all my self restraint. Plastering on a smile, I reply. "Of course. You're probably exhausted. Shirts are in the second drawer. I'll just be out here if you need me."

As Sara enters the bedroom, she glances over her shoulder. "Goodnight, Mitch."

CHAPTER TEN

I can't sleep. How can I when I'm surrounded by Mitch's scent? His sheets smell like a mix of his citrus body wash and his natural sea salt aroma.

I should be thinking about ways to get back home, but when we were walking here, I could see the dome above us and the vast sea above that. I'm certainly not getting home on my own, and if the rumors surrounding the Bermuda Triangle are true—which it seems like they are—then I'm stuck here for the foreseeable future.

And honestly, what is there for me to go back for, anyway? To prove to my family I'm smart and successful? Will they even care? Almost dying has apparently shifted my perspective on what's important in life.

Right now, what's important is sleep, and I won't be getting any without some relief. The ache between my thighs has just gotten worse the longer I've laid here. I know Mitch is just on the other side of the door and he'd jump at the chance to come join me if I asked him. I'm not blind. I saw him adjust himself more than a couple times on our walk home. From what Martha and Layla told me, he will be a horny mess until we complete the bond.

I've read enough of those shifter romance novels to know that means doing the nasty. Shit, if there are eel shifters, are wolf shifters real, too? Do eel shifters have knots? I wonder what their cocks look like.

Knowing I won't get any sleep while I'm worked up like this, I give in. Dragging my fingertips up my thighs, I graze the lips of my sex and realize I'm already dripping, making a mess of Mitch's sheets. Sliding up, I reach my breasts, pinching a nipple hard with each hand. There is no taking it slow right now. When I pinch them again. I have to turn my head into the pillow to stifle my moan.

I *need* to come. One hand drops down to my pussy, first spreading myself wide to feel the cool air of the room hit my wet center. Using my other hand, I roll my clit between my thumb and forefinger, unable to control the gasp that escapes me. Hopefully Mitchell is asleep by now, but even if he isn't, there is no way I'm stopping.

Impatient, I thrust two fingers inside my pussy and start rocking my hips, imagining it's Mitch who is letting me ride his hand. Needing more, I slide in a third finger and relish the burn of the stretch. Imagining it's Mitchell's cock thrusting in and out of me instead of my fingers has me so close I could scream. Curling my body for leverage, I add another finger and fuck myself hard. The heel of my palm presses against my clit and I explode. I barely hold in a scream of pleasure, but a deep moan fills the room.

How the hell am I still horny? After coming harder than I have in months, I should be passed the fuck out. Instead, my body is buzzing, my pussy throbbing and clenching around nothing. When the nurses explained the mating frenzy to me, I nodded politely but shrugged it off. I guess I should have listened. Mitch has been fighting this feeling for days? Nice to know my supposed mate has the self restraint of a gladiator, but I don't. Fuck this.

Whipping off the covers, I stomp to the door, flinging it open, startling Mitch on the couch. "Sara? Is everything ok?" He starts to sit up, but before he can, I'm straddling him, pushing his chest to get him to lie back down. A roll of my hips has him gripping my hips tightly, thrusting up slightly to meet my core. Then my lips are on his, devouring him with no finesse. Sitting up with me still on his lap, he shoves his hands into my hair, gripping the strands firmly. Tugging my head back, he breaks the kiss.

"Sara, what? What is happening right now?"

"You aren't a virgin, right, Mitch?" He shakes his head. "Didn't think so. You should know what's about to happen right now." He throws his head back over the couch as I grind my cunt against his hard cock. Just because I can't kiss him doesn't mean I can't drive him crazy in other ways. His pelvis lifts, involuntarily seeking pleasure.

"Sara, ungh fuck. Are you—fuuuck. Oh shit, wait." Mitch stutters as I continue my ministrations. Why the fuck is he fighting this?

"Mitch. The nice ladies at the emergency center told me all about the mating frenzy. I know what's happening. *Now, fuck me.*"

His eyes darken and he uses his grip on my head to crush me against him, his restraint snapping. We're still clothed, though, and that needs to change ASAP. Pulling off his lips, I slide to my knees and reach for the waistband of his joggers. He lifts his ass so I can free his hard cock, rising on my knees and closing my eyes as I take his tip into my mouth. My tongue swirls around until it hits something. Popping off his cock, I sit back to inspect it. Holy hell, that's new.

CHAPTER ELEVEN

Mitchell

"What is *that*?" Not exactly what a man wants to hear from his woman when she was about to suck his soul out through his cock, but I know what she's asking about.

"It's my frill. It's normal for Eelkin, I promise." My voice is tight.

"Can I touch it?" She asks.

I groan. "Please, fuck, yes."

Sara has been surprising me since I met her, so of course my feisty mate doesn't run her fingers along it. No, she leans forward and licks the underside of my cock from my balls to tip, her tongue trailing my frill.

"Jesus Fuck!" I shout. I've never felt anything like it. I knew it was sensitive, but this is a whole new level. Mischief sparkles in her eyes before she takes my cock in her mouth and nearly swallows me whole. My hands fly to the couch cushions, bracing myself against the pleasure as she bobs on my dick.

"Sara, baby, stop or I'm gonna—" Instead of stopping, she doubles down, swallowing my cock so far down her throat that her nose hits my pubic bone, exactly like I fantasized. My hands fly up to her head, holding her to me as I spill warm cum down her throat. When I finish, she pops off and licks her lips, staring at my cock wide-eyed.

"You're still hard?" She questions. And yeah, by human standards that would be unusual. But the mating frenzy is in full swing so normal rules don't apply.

Giving her a wicked smile, I lean forward, crashing into her and pinning her to the floor, making sure to put my hand behind her head to cushion her fall. She's in nothing but my shirt and her panties. Burrowing my face in her neck, I lick and bite her sensitive skin, bring my hands up to knead her full breasts, stimulating her taut nipples through the thin cotton. Mapping her body with my lips, open mouth kisses bringing me to her tits. Unable to resist, I push up the fabric to suck the tight buds into my mouth, laving each one until she's squirming, begging me with her pants and moans for more.

The sweet scent of her arousal is calling my name, though, so I quickly move lower, settling her calves over my shoulders and placing a sharp bite on her inner thigh. She's so wet, her panties are ruined, damp fabric clinging to her, revealing the cleft of her pussy. The mating frenzy is impatient. I waste no time pushing the fabric to the side and burying my face in her cunt.

"Ahh! Mitchell! Fuck!" Sara jerks her hips, but I wrap my arms around her thighs, pulling her tighter to my mouth, devouring her like she's my last meal. Her cum drips down her folds while I alternate between sucking her clit and licking up every drop from her entrance. "Please, please, please, please!" She's gorgeous when she begs and I find I can't deny her. Shifting slightly, I free my right arm and shove two fingers inside her. Hitting no resistance, I pull my hand back to add a third finger to her pussy. My left arm's still wrapped around her leg, but I stretch and use my hand to push down right above her pubic bone while my pumping fingers rub the rough patch on her inner wall.

"Fuck, baby, you taste so good. You like my fingers stretching this pretty cunt, getting you ready for my cock?"

She mewls as her walls clench my fingers so tight they are nearly pushed out. Squirming, her alarmed eyes meet mine. "Wait! It feels like I have to pee...what—"

I cut her off. "Have you ever squirted, Sara?" She shakes her head and excitement fills me. "You're about to, baby. Push through it." Rubbing her g-spot harder, I dip down to suck on her clit and this time her pussy clenches so hard my fingers are forced out of her. "Fuck yes, give it to me." Sweetness gushes onto my face and into my mouth as her orgasm hits her like a freight train and she squirts for the first time. I nearly come again from the experience, knowing I was the first to push her that high.

Sara is panting, looking at me like I'm from another planet—and it isn't because of my Eelkin form, I'm sure of it.

"Do you want to stop?" I ask. Fuck knows I want nothing more that to bury myself in her warm body, but that probably took a lot out of her. Her expression morphs from awe to indignation.

"Fuck no, I don't want to stop!"

"Thank fuck." Before I can move, Sarah rolls to her stomach, pushing up on her knees and spreading her thighs in invitation. Not going to question her again, she's made it very clear. Slotting myself behind her, I drag my cockhead through her folds twice, then enter her in one hard thrust.

CHAPTER TWELVE

This mating frenzy is no joke. I was skeptical at first, but I have never been this turned on for this long before. Mitchell doesn't hesitate, pounding me hard, skin slapping each time he bottoms out. The frills on his cock are like nothing I've ever experienced. I've been with men who were pierced, child's play compared to what Mitch has going on.

He's panting my name, praises falling from his lips as he takes his pleasure like a wild animal. A hand smooths down my back and I think he wants me to lower my face to the floor, but he surprises me by threading strong fingers into my hair and pulling back. My back arches and he is hitting even deeper than before.

"Sara, I'm too close. Come again for me. I need it," Mitchell begs breathlessly while I shake my head. I really don't think I have it in me. Suddenly he pulls me up, pinning me to his chest, snaking one hand between my breasts and up to my throat, his hold firm yet gentle as he locks his fingers under my jaw. His other hand snakes around my hip, but he doesn't assault my clit like I think he will. He cups my sex as he growls in my ear.

"Yes, you can. You're gonna give me one more. I want to follow you over that cliff and fill you with my cum. Can I come in you, Sara?"

Fuck, that's hot. Unable to nod, I'm forced to say it out loud, which is what I think he wants. "Yes! Come in me. I want it." A sharp slap lands on my clit and I'm lost, coming hard and long, Mitchell thrusting erratically through his orgasm as his cum fills me.

After what feels like ages, we both come back to earth, covered in sweat and cum and god knows what else. Mitchell slides out of me, our combined release dripping from my used pussy. Scooping me up, he heads toward the shower.

I can hear the grin in his voice. "Let's get cleaned up, baby. This mating frenzy is just getting started."

EPILOGUE

Cool water caresses my skin as I slip into the shallows. I've never been skinny dipping before, but I couldn't refuse when Mitch trained those bright green eyes on me, pleading with me without words. Not that I would have turned him down. It feels wrong, and risky, and I love it. He took us down to the beaches by the caves, the only light the ethereal bioluminescent glow.

Mitch slides in beside me, then grabs my hand and drags me further in the water, just around a small outcropping of rocks. We're hidden out of obvious sight, but someone could still see us if they were at the right angle.

Life in Ankaria has been...interesting. Not bad, obviously. Who wouldn't want to live in an underwater paradise with a mate that spoils you both in and out of bed? I don't think it'll ever stop being kinda weird, though. It's only been six months, maybe once a year passes I'll be jaded to it all.

Scales softly scrape my bare skin as Mitch presses against me, trapping me between his body and the rocks.

Right to the good stuff, huh? You won't see me complaining. His mouth moves slowly on mine, not a fevered rush but a sensual dance of our lips and tongues. My hands grip his shoulders. I love the feeling of his armor-like scales.

Mitch's hands stop caressing my breasts to slide down my body, one reaching around to grip my ass as he slides two fingers inside me with the other. Usually our mating is fast and furious, but something about how much time he's taking, as if he has all the time in the world, has me burning with arousal. He plays my body like his own personal instrument, unerringly finding my g-spot every single damn time. Gripping my ass harder, he holds me in place as his fingers speed up, slamming in and out of me until I'm biting his shoulder to muffle the sound of my climax.

He slips his fingers out of me, but when I think he's going to wrap my legs around him so he can fuck me, he makes sure I'm gripping the rocks and then slips away. I nearly whine at the loss until he gives me a wicked grin and slips below the water. Oh shit, is he gonna...

I startle when something slick brushes my legs with intention. Mitch has taken his eel form and is doing figure eights around my calves like a cat begging for attention. He was pleased to discover that he regained his eel form when he found me, his mate.

He makes his way past my knees, continuing his pattern around my thighs now. I'm panting, fingers gripping the rocks behind me to keep from slipping under the water, when he slips away. Suddenly, a featherlite stroke of what must be his tail drags across my legs, followed by a tingling feeling.

Oh fuck. We've talked about this before. I've never tried electric play, but the idea has always been intriguing. But a violet wand doesn't have half the shock power an electric eel can generate, which makes Mitch far riskier to play with. People talk about the thrill of primal play, the idea that a predator could hurt you, even kill you, driving the experience to new heights.

Well, they haven't tried it with an eel shifter. Not only is the knowledge that he's dangerous ramping up my adrenaline, but I can't see him. I never know where he's coming from, or where the zaps from his tail and fins will land on my skin.

He varies the power and pressure on each stroke of my breasts, thighs, and stomach, until I'm desperate. He slithers his way down my back and over my ass, pressing against the gap in my thighs, seeking entry. Taking a deep breath, I open to him, and he swims through to the front and back around, warning me what's about to happen. On the next pass, he adds a little electricity, tingling the outside of my pussy. It feels so much better than I imagined after all the foreplay, and I spread my legs further. On his third pass, he presses tighter to my body, delivering a slightly stronger shock straight to my swollen clit.

"Holy fucking mother of pearl...shit...ah! Fuckity fuck... fuck!"

I'm not proud of the expletives that come sailing out of my mouth, but I really don't have control over it any more. All my brain power has been used up by the most epic orgasm probably in the history of orgasms. No thoughts, only pleasure.

I nearly lose my grip and slip into the water, but then Mitch is there in his eelkin form, holding my legs open and thrusting his frilled cock deep inside me. He slams into me over and over again, and I can tell he's on the edge. Just a few more powerful thrusts and he's coming, burying his face in my neck.

"I love you, Sara. I love you so fucking much." His proclamation sends me over the edge once more, my cunt milking every last drop of his release from his pulsing cock.

For a moment, we just hold each other. I stroke his back in soothing patterns as we come back down to Earth. When we are breathing normally again, I gently push his shoulders, prompting Mitch to pull back enough that I can meet his gaze.

"You know that wasn't fair, springing that on me when I was so turned on I couldn't talk." I tease.

"Oh? Do you need me to say it again?" He replies. "Because I will, as many times as you'll let me. Sara, I lo—"

I place a finger to his lips to cut him off. "I love you, too...Mitcharoonie."

His dopey, lovestruck expression morphs into exasperation before we both erupt into laughter. If this is what being an eel shifter's mate means—-loving, laughing, and fucking —then I'm definitely ready to sign up for forever.

Thank you so much for reading *Slip into Me*! This whole thing started with my husband explaining how no one has ever seen eels breed in the wild. They just pop off to the Sargasso Sea, adult eels go in and baby eels come out. I hope you enjoyed this steamy short, and if you want more unusual monsters and unique omegaverse, be sure to check out my Instagram (instagram.com/cloverhollowayauthor) for the most up-to-date info.

ACKNOWLEDGEMENTS

Thank you for reading *Slip into Me*! I may have written this story as Clover, but this book was written while I was at the beginning of my insane Unfortunate Reads journey. I have so many people to thank who have been integral to getting me to this point, but there are a few I especially want to mention.

Thank you to the many authors in Latrexa Nova's discord server who encouraged me to enter the Contest of Coital Chaos despite the fact I had never written anything for publication before. Most importantly, thank you Vera Valentine, Latrexa Nova, and Sylvia Morrow for beta reading, editing, and fighting my impostor syndrome one panic attack at a time. Five hundred words sounds like an easy task, but writing a satisfying story with spice and sentient objects in what is essentially a paragraph is actually hard as shit. Without my book friends, I probably wouldn't have submitted anything.

The cadre of sentient object romance authors, or the SORority as we have taken to calling it, is one of the most inclusive, kind, encouraging communities I have ever been a part of.

Thank you to the ladies of Dark Village Publishing (whom I met via Unfortunate Reads), for encouraging me to lengthen the clock story and submit it to their anthology. And thank you to all my followers who jumped to read that story SO fast. I was truly shocked.

I'd also like to give a heartfelt thanks to Thea Masen. She was the first person to approach me about doing a co-write, and who, along with Kate McDarris, convinced me my writing was good enough for something like that. Thea, thank you for constantly helping me battle that pesky impostor syndrome, and thank you in advance for continuing to do so. 😆

Marcella (poetry_drive), I can't even remember how we ended up in each other's DMs, but I am so thankful it happened. I appreciate your support, beta reading, brainstorming, reviewing, memes, trauma dump listening, and general badassery more than you could ever know.

It seems inadequate to thank my beta readers, because in reality I consider Danelle (biblio.barbie), Nicole Parker, Amber (buzzcutbiblio), and Dakota Cockaday amazing friends. Thank you for always *immediately* jumping on whatever bullshit I write, whether it's a story about a monstera man, or the ocean throwing cod at a chick's airbnb.

Thank you to my ARC team (absolutely wild that I have an ARC team now) for being down to read and hype up anything. Your DMs and reviews make me smile *every single time*. Sorry I keep sending you things, like, a week before they publish. I'd like to say I'll change, but I'm 37 and if I haven't gotten my shit together by now, chances are this is just who I am. Thank you all for rolling with it.

I have always avoided doing specific acknowledgements due to the fear of forgetting to include someone, but if you've been a part of my journey, just know I'm grateful. That includes all of you who picked up this book. As indie authors, every purchase, review, quote highlight, and comment matters. Thank you all for lifting us up over and over again. A million virtual hugs to all of you!

Stay lucky,
🍀 Clover

About the Author

Clover Holloway is the sweeter side of Unfortunate Reads, writing steamy monster and omegaverse romance that will leave you swooning and sweating.

A long time romance reader turned author, she just can't help but make her stories cozy. She's an ADHD agent of chaos, so her book topics may vary wildly, but you can always expect an HEA. She's an avid fan of traditional millennial customs including craft breweries, monstera plants, and skinny jeans.

You can find all her links at cloverholloway.com, including her Patreon, which is shared with Unfortunate Reads so you get two for one.

Stay lucky!

cloverholloway.com

Also by Author

By Clover Holloway

Monstera (re-release coming soon)

Zero to 69 *(co-write with Thea Masen & Kate McDarris)*

Welcome to Bone Town *(co-write with Thea Masen)*

By Unfortunate Reads

Handle Me

Pushin' Cushions *(co-write with Vera Valentine)*

Fully Charged *(co-write with Nicole Parker)*

Santa's Sack *(co-write with Nicole Parker)*

Sentient Object Holiday Shared Series

My Date With Water

My Date With a Jellyfish